50+ Greatest Intermediate Classics for Recorder

Over 50 favourite melodies from the world's greatest composers arranged especially for recorder

Amanda Oosthuizen

Jemima Oosthuizen

The Ruby Recorder Series

Wild Music Publications
www.wildmusicpublications.com

We hope you enjoy *50+ Greatest Intermediate Classics for Recorder!*

Take a look at other exciting recorder books.
Including: *Wicked Duets, Sea Shanties and Songs, Christmas Crackers, Trick or Treat – A Halloween Suite, More Christmas Duets, 40+ Country Dances, Fun Folk for Fun Folk, Little Gems for Recorder and Piano, Moonlight and Roses, Fish 'n' Ships, Intermediate Classic Duets, 50+ Greatest Classics for Recorder, The Ruby Recorder Book of Music Theory (especially for recorder players), Recorder Practice Notebook* and many more!

For more info on other amazing books, please go to:

WildMusicPublications.com

Happy Tooting!

To keep up to date with our new releases, why not **follow us on Twitter?**

@WMPublications

Wild Music Publications

ISBN 978-1-914510-27-4

Contents

Adagio – Albinoni 9

Alla Turca, *Piano Concerto – Mozart* 29

Autumn, *The Four Seasons – Vivaldi* 2

Ave Maria – Schubert 35

Bist du bei mir – Stölzel 11

Caprice – Paganini 45

Carol of the Bells – Leontovych 6

Clog Dance, *La fille mal gardée* - Hertel 58

Colonel Bogey – Alford 12

Csárdás – Monti 32

Donauwellen Waltz – Ivanovici 42

Danse macabre – Saint Saëns 36

Entry of the Gladiators – Fučík 24

Frühlingsstimmen – J. Strauss 34

Funiculì, Funiculà – Denza 4

Für Elise – Beethoven 62

Garland Waltz, *Sleeping Beauty* – Tchaikovsky 20

Gliding Dance of the Maidens, *Polovtsian Dances* – Borodin 8

Gran Valse – Tárrega 54

Hungarian Dance No. 5 – Brahms 10

La Campanella, *Violin Concerto – Paganini* 40

Lacrimosa, *Requiem – Mozart* 50

Largo al Factotum, *Barber of Seville* – Rossini 68

Light Cavalry Overture – Suppé 61

Marche Funèbre – Gounod 30

Marche Slave – Tchaikovsky 44

Mazurka, *Op. 7, No. 1* – Chopin 52

Moonlight Sonata – Beethoven 65

Nimrod, *Enigma Variations* – Elgar.............................7

Nocturne – Chopin 57

Overture, *Le Nozze di Figaro* – Mozart.............................69

Pizzicati, *Sylvia* - Delibes.............................64

Prelude, *Carmen*– Bizet.............................38

Rigaudon, *Holberg Suite* – Grieg 60

Romanze, *Eine Kleine Nachtmusik* – Mozart 26

Russian Dance, *Nutcracker Suite* – Tchaikovsky.............................33

Sarabande, *Suite in D minor* – Handel 14

Scheherazade, *Suite Symphonique* – Rimsky-Korsakov 53

Sheep May Safely Graze – J. S. Bach 41

Si un jour, *La forza del destino* – Verdi 15

Sleepers, Awake, *Choral Cantata* – J.S. Bach.............................59

Ständchen, *Schwanengesang* – Schubert 23

Te Deum – Charpentier 3

Theme, *Pastoral Symphony* – Beethoven.............................19

Theme, *Piano Concerto No. 1* – Tchaikovsky 28

Three Little Maids, *The Mikado* – Sullivan 56

Toccata and Fugue – J.S Bach.............................48

Traümerai, *Reverie* – Schumann 39

Tritsch Tratsch Polka – J. Strauss 16

Valse – Chopin 46

Va, Pensiero, *Nabucco* – Verdi.............................22

Vltava, *Ma Vlast* – Smetana 17

Waltz no. 15 – Brahms.............................18

Information

Tempo and Expression Markings

Adagio – slow and stately

agitato – excited, agitated

Allegretto – moderately fast

Allegro – fast and bright

Andante – at walking speed

Andante quasi allegretto – faster than *Andante*

Andante sostenuto – a little slower than *Andante*

Andantino – slightly faster (or sometimes slower) than *Andante*

brillante – spirited and sparkling

cantando – in a singing style

commodo – comfortably fast

con anima – in a spirited manner

con brio – with vigour

con espressione – with expression

dolce – sweetly

giocoso – cheerful

grazioso – gracefully

Grave solemn and slow

Largamente – slow and broad

Largo – slow and stately

Maestoso – majestically

ma non troppo – but not too much

Moderato - moderately

in modo di marcia funebre – like a funeral march

nobilmente – nobly

piacevole – pleasant and agreeable

Poco moto – with movement but not too fast

Presto – extremely fast

Prestissimo – very quickly

Rinforzando – with increasing emphasis

Solenne – solemn and grave

Sostenuto – sustained

sotto voce – a dramatic lowering of volume

Vivace – lively and fast

Vivo – lively and brisk

a tempo – in time (or return to original speed)

accel. – accelerando – get gradually faster

rall. – rallentando – gradually slowing down

rit. – ritenuto – get slightly slower

ritard. – ritardando – get gradually slower

al fine – to the end

 fermata – pause on this note

dim. – diminuendo – gradually softer

cresc. – crescendo – gradually louder

pp – *pianissimo* – very softly

p – *piano* – softly

mp – *mezzo piano* moderately soft

mf – *mezzo forte* – moderately loud

f – *forte* – loud

ff – *fortissimo* – very loud

fff *fortississimo* – very, very loud

fp – *fortepiano* – loud then immediately soft

sf – *subito forte* – suddenly loud

rf – *rinforzando* – with increasing emphasis

fz – forzando – forced beyond the usual dynamic for the passage

ffz – as above but stronger

sfz – *sforzando* – suddenly forced

gradually getting softer

gradually getting louder

Articulation

 staccato – short and detached

leggiero – play lightly

accent – played with attack

tenuto – held– pressured accent

marcato – forcefully

Ornaments

 trill – rapid movement to the note above and back or from the note above in Mozart and earlier music.

mordent – three rapid notes – the principal note, the note above and the principal.

 acciaccatura – a very quick note

 appoggiatura – divide the main note equally between the two notes.

Autumn

from *The Four Seasons*

Antonio Vivaldi
(1678-1741)

Te Deum

Marc-Antoine Charpentier
(1643-1704)

Funiculì, Funiculà

Luigi Denza
(1846-1922)

Allegro brilliante

p   *grazioso.*

pp   *cresc.*

f   *pp*   *f*

mp   *p*

pp

Carol of the Bells

Ukranian Bell Carol

Mykola Leontovych
(1877-1921)

Nimrod

from *Enigma Variations*

Edward Elgar
(1857-1934)

Gliding Dance of the Maidens

from *Polovtsian Dances, Prince Igor*

Alexander Borodin
(1833-1887)

Adagio

Tomaso Albinoni
(1671-1751)

Hungarian Dance No. 5

Johannes Brahms
(1833-1897)

Bist du bei mir

from *A Little Notebook for Anna Magdalena*

Gottfried Heinrich Stölzel
(1690-1749)
attrib. Johann Sebastian Bach

Colonel Bogey March

Kenneth J. Alford
(1881-1945)

Quick march

12

Sarabande

from *Suite in D minor*

George Frideric Handel
(1685-1759)

Si un jour

from *La forza del destino*

Guiseppe Verdi
(1813-1901)

Tritsch-Tratsch Polka

Opus 214

Johann Strauss
(1825-1899)

Molto Allegro

Vltava

from *Má vlast*

Bedřich Smetana
(1824-1884)

Allegro comodo non agitato

Waltz No. 15

Johannes Brahms
(1833-1897)

Theme

from *Symphony No. 6 'Pastoral'*

Ludvig van Beethoven
(1770-1827)

Garland Waltz

from *Sleeping Beauty*

Pyotr Ilyich Tchaikovsky
(1840-1893)

Va, pensiero

Chorus of the Hebrew Slaves
from *Nabucco*

Guiseppe Verdi
(1813-1901)

Ständchen

from *Schwanengesang*

Franz Schubert
(1797-1828)

Entry of the Gladiators

Julius Ernest Wilhelm Fučík
(1872-1916)

Romanze

from *Eine Kleine Nachtmusik*

Wolfgang Amadeus Mozart
(1756-1791)

Theme

from *Piano Concerto No. 1 in B flat minor*

Pyotr Ilyich Tchaikovsky
(1840-1893)

Andante non troppo e molto maestoso

Alla Turca

from *Piano Sonata No. 11*

Wolfgang Amadeus Mozart
(1756-1791)

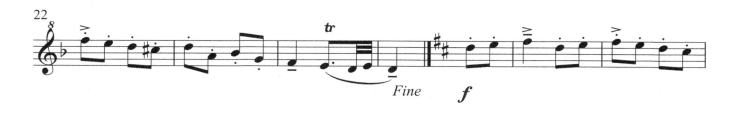

D.C al Fine

Marche funèbre d'une marionnette

Charles Gounod
(1818-1893)

Csárdás

Vittorio Monti
(1868-1922)

Russian Dance

Trepak from *The Nutcracker Suite*

Pyotr Ilyich Tchaikovsky
(1840-1893)

Molto vivace

Frühlingsstimmen

Rêve de printemps - Voices of Spring

Opus 410

Johann Strauss
(1825-1899)

Ave Maria

Op. 52, No. 6

Franz Schubert
(1797-1828)

Andante

Danse macabre

Camille Saint-Saëns
(1835-1921)

38

Prelude

from Carmen

Georges Bizet
(1838-1875)

Träumerei

Reverie from *Op. 15, No. 7*

Robert Schumann
(1810-1856)

La Campanella

from *Violin Concerto No. 2*

Niccolo Paganini
(1782-1840)

Allegro moderato

Sheep may safely graze

from *Cantata BWV 208*

Johann Sebastian Bach
(1685-1750)

Donauwellen Walzer

Waves of the Danube Waltz

Iosif Ivanovici
(1845-1902)

Marche Slave

Opus 31

Pyotr Ilyich Tchaikovsky
(1840-1893)

Moderato in modo di marcia funebre

Caprice

Niccolo Paganini
(1782-1840)

Valse

Frédéric Chopin
(1810-1849)

Toccata and Fugue

Johann Sebastian Bach
(1685-1750)

Lacrimosa

from *Requiem in D minor*

Wolfgang Amadeus Mozart
(1756-1791)

Mazurka

from *Op. 7, No. 1*

Frédéric Chopin
(1810-1849)

Scheherazade

from *Suite Symphonique Op. 35*

Nikolai Rimsky-Korsakov
(1844-1908)

Gran Valse

Francisco Tárrega
(1852-1909)

Three Little Maids

from *The Mikado*

Arthur Seymour Sullivan
(1842-1900)

Allegretto grazioso

Nocturne

Frédéric Chopin
(1810-1849)

Clog Dance

from *La fille mal gardée*

Peter Ludwig Hertel
(1817-1899)

Sleepers, Awake!

from choral cantata *Wachet auf, ruft uns die Stimme BWV 140*

Johann Sebastian Bach
(1685-1750)

Rigaudon

from *Holberg Suite*

Edvard Grieg
(1843-1907)

Light Cavalry Overture

Franz von Suppé
(1819-1895)

Allegro brilliante

Für Elise

Ludwig van Beethoven
(1770-1827)

Pizzicati

from *Sylvia*

Léo Delibes
(1836-1891)

Moonlight Sonata

Movement 1 Op. 27 No. 2

Ludwig van Beethoven
(1770-1827)

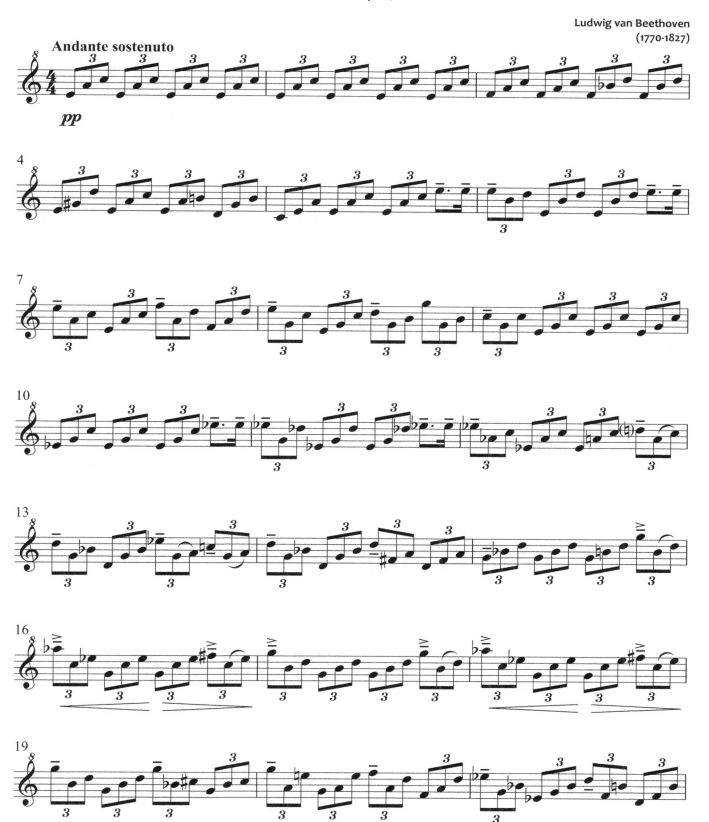

66

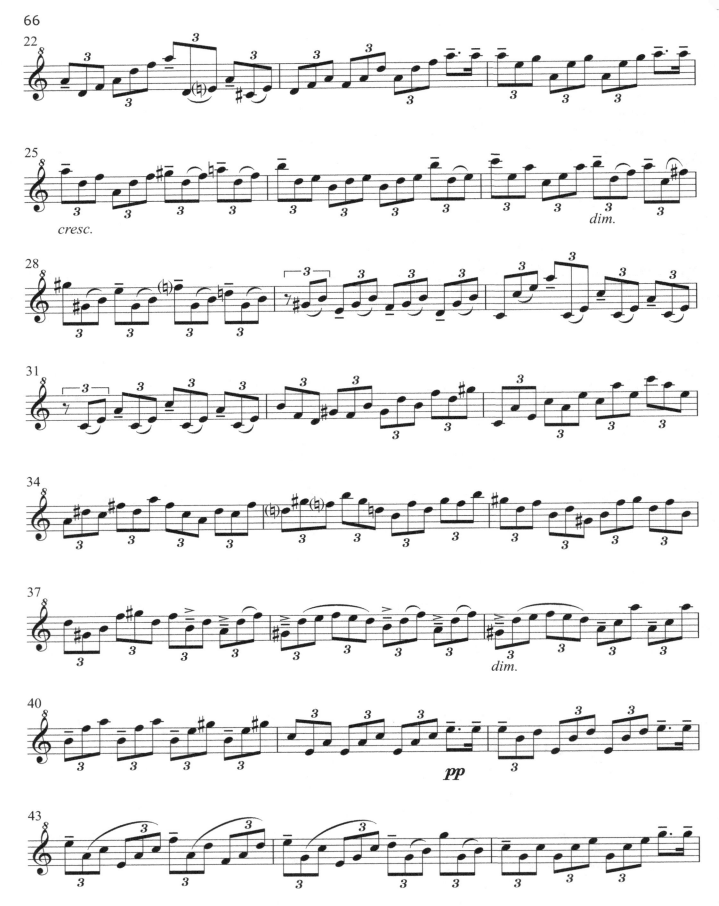

Largo al factotum

from *The Barber of Seville*

Gioacchino Rossini
(1792-1868)

Overture

from *Le nozze di Figaro*

Wolfgang Amadeus Mozart
(1756-1791)

If you have enjoyed **50+ Greatest Intermediate Classics for Recorder,** why not try the other books in the **Ruby Recorder** series!

For more info, please visit: **WildMusicPublications.com**

All of our books are available to download, or you can order from Amazon.

Introducing some of our favourites:

Intermediate Classic Duets

Christmas Crackers

Sea Shanties and Songs

Wicked Duets

More Fun Folk for Fun Folk

Champagne and Chocolate

Learn Recorder through Famous Classics

Christmas Duets

Christmas Trios

47870921R00044